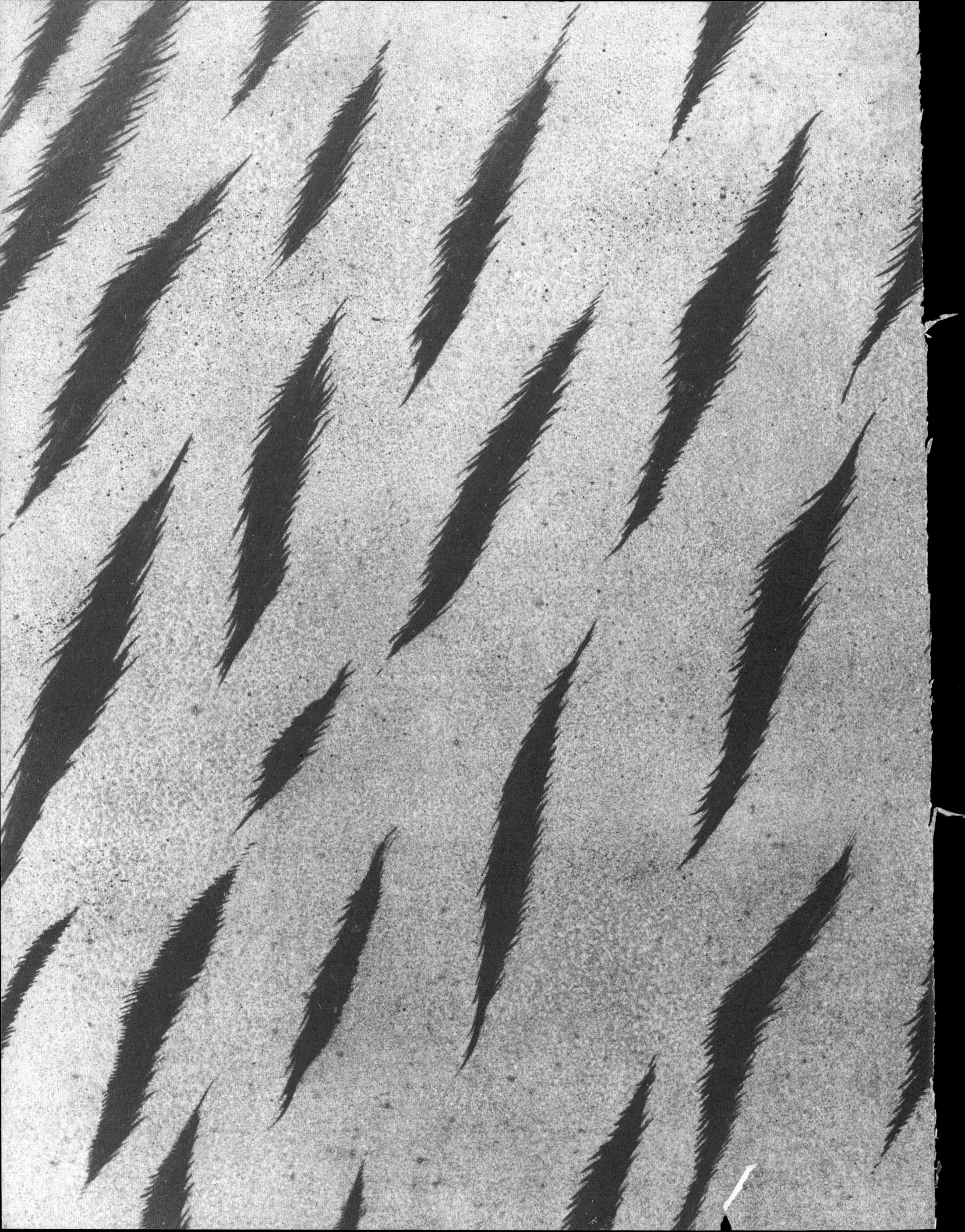

THE BIG PETS

by Lane Smith

VIKING

VIKING
Published by the Penguin Group
Viking Penguin, a division of Penguin Books USA Inc.
375 Hudson Street, New York, New York 10014, U.S.A.
Penguin Books Ltd, 27 Wrights Lane, London W8 5TZ, England
Penguin Books Australia Ltd, Ringwood, Victoria, Australia
Penguin Books Canada Ltd, 2801 John Street, Markham, Ontario, Canada L3R 1B4
Penguin Books (N.Z.) Ltd, 182–190 Wairau Road, Auckland 10, New Zealand

Penguin Books Ltd, Registered Offices: Harmondsworth, Middlesex, England

First published in 1991 by Viking Penguin, a division of Penguin Books USA Inc.

10 9 8 7 6 5 4 3 2 1

Library of Congress Cataloging in Publication Data
Smith, Lane. The big pets / by Lane Smith. p. cm.
Summary: A little girl explores the mysterious dreamworld where small children play with their big pets, which range from cats and dogs to snakes and crickets.
[1. Animals—Fiction. 2. Pets—Fiction. 3. Dreams—Fiction.] I. Title.
PZ7.S6538Bi 1991 [E]—dc20 ISBN 0-670-8 90-42047 CIP

Printed in Japan Set in Weiss

Design: Molly Leach, New York, New York.

To Sarah, Amy and Kyle
—L.S.

The girl was small and the cat was big.

And on certain nights
she rode on his back
to the place where
the Milk-Pool was.

While he drank,
she swam.
And she came out
smelling like
fresh milk.

So did the other night children who gathered there.

The big cat would lick off the extra, then he and the girl walked about, drying her hair in the warm night breeze.

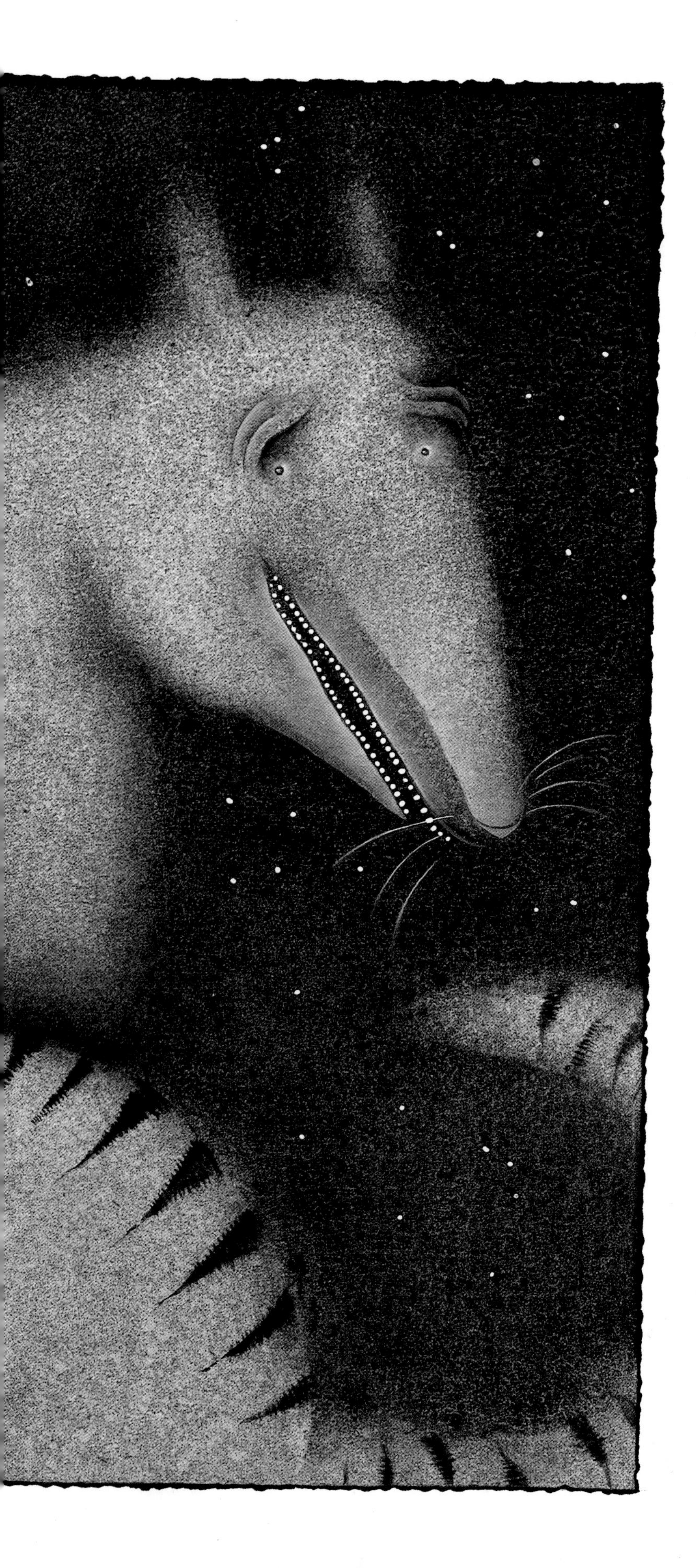

Sometimes they saw
the small boy
who rode on the back
of the big dog.
And they waved
as he headed
for the Bone Gardens.

There, he played while his dog gnawed.

Together, they dug up old bones with
other kids who came with their dogs.

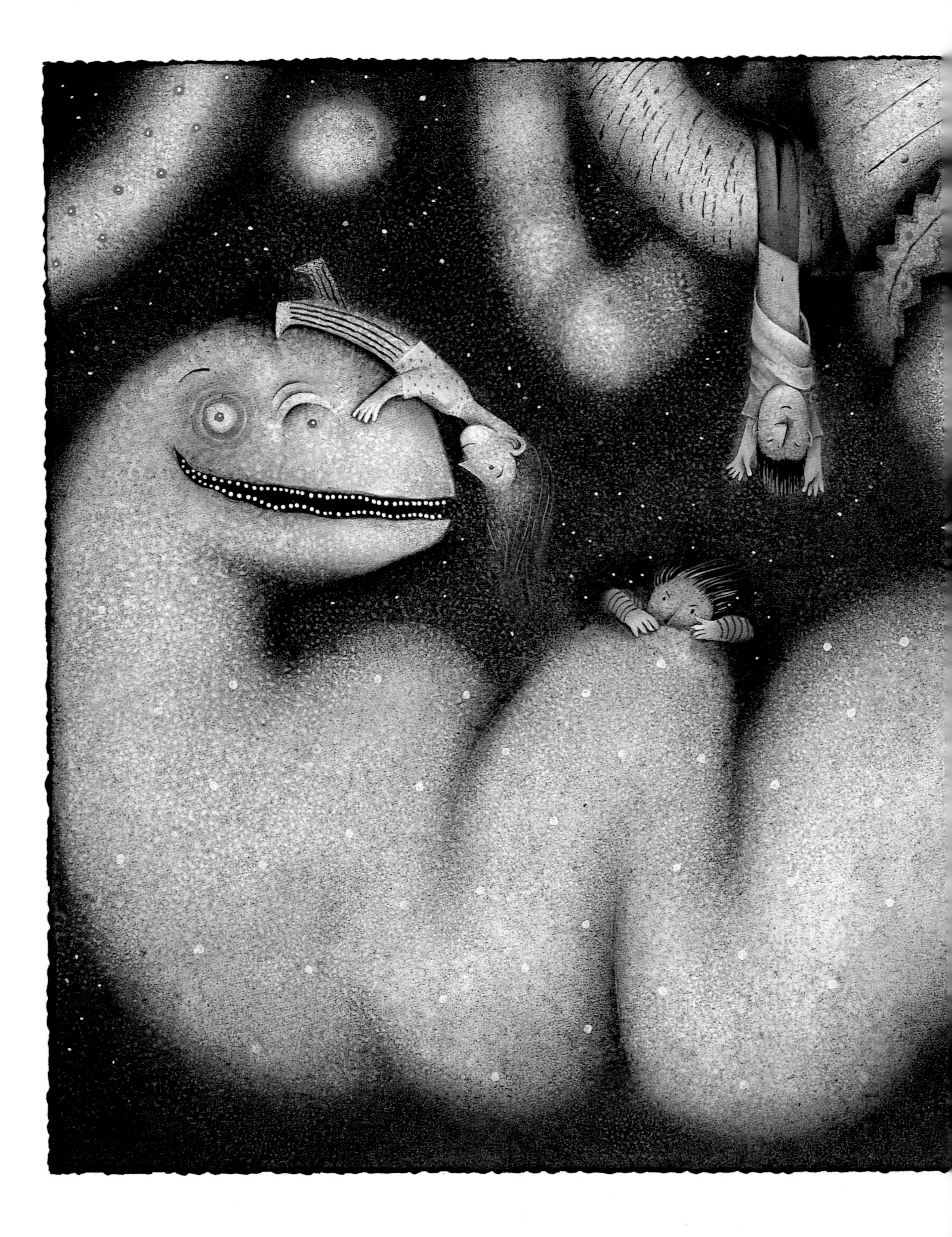

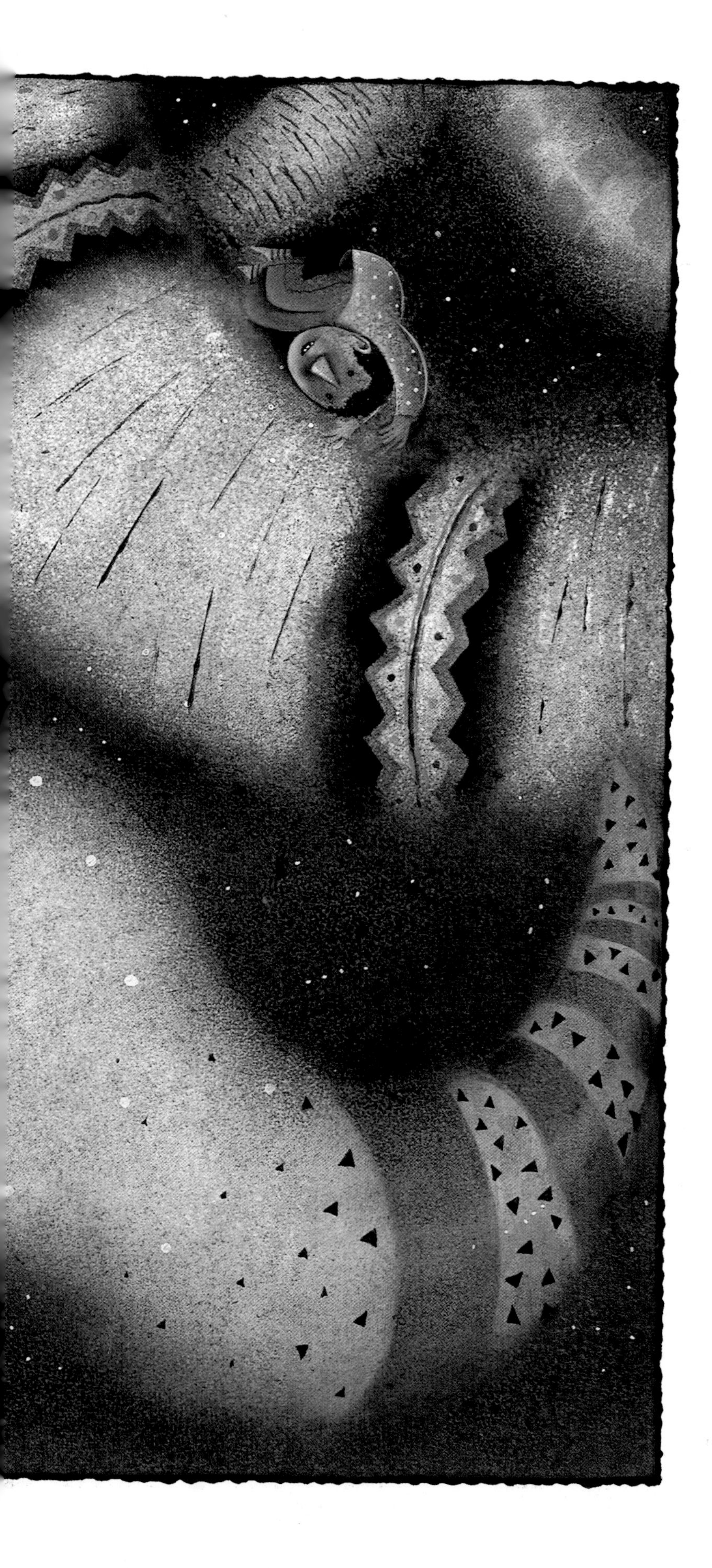

A mile away
at the Grassy Plains,
a dozen kids,
sometimes more,
rolled and tumbled
with their pet snakes.

And a little
beyond that,
children played
at the Hamster Holes.

And at Cricket Creek one little boy sat with his pet.

The cat and the girl often wondered what fun there was in that.
Especially, when one could easily wish for a Milk-Pool...

or a Scratching Forest...

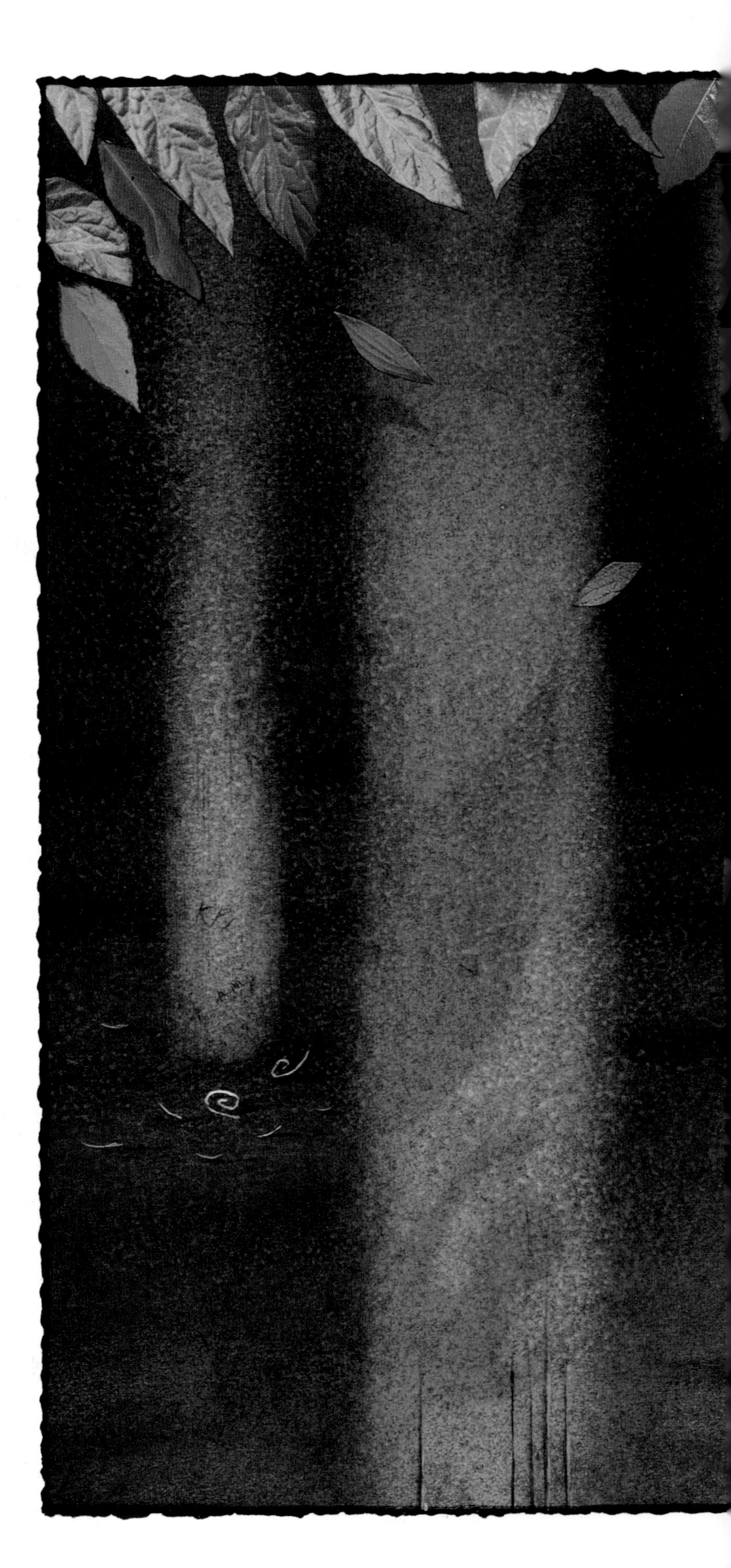

or a place where the Stringy Vines teased.

And if one were truly lucky, perhaps even...

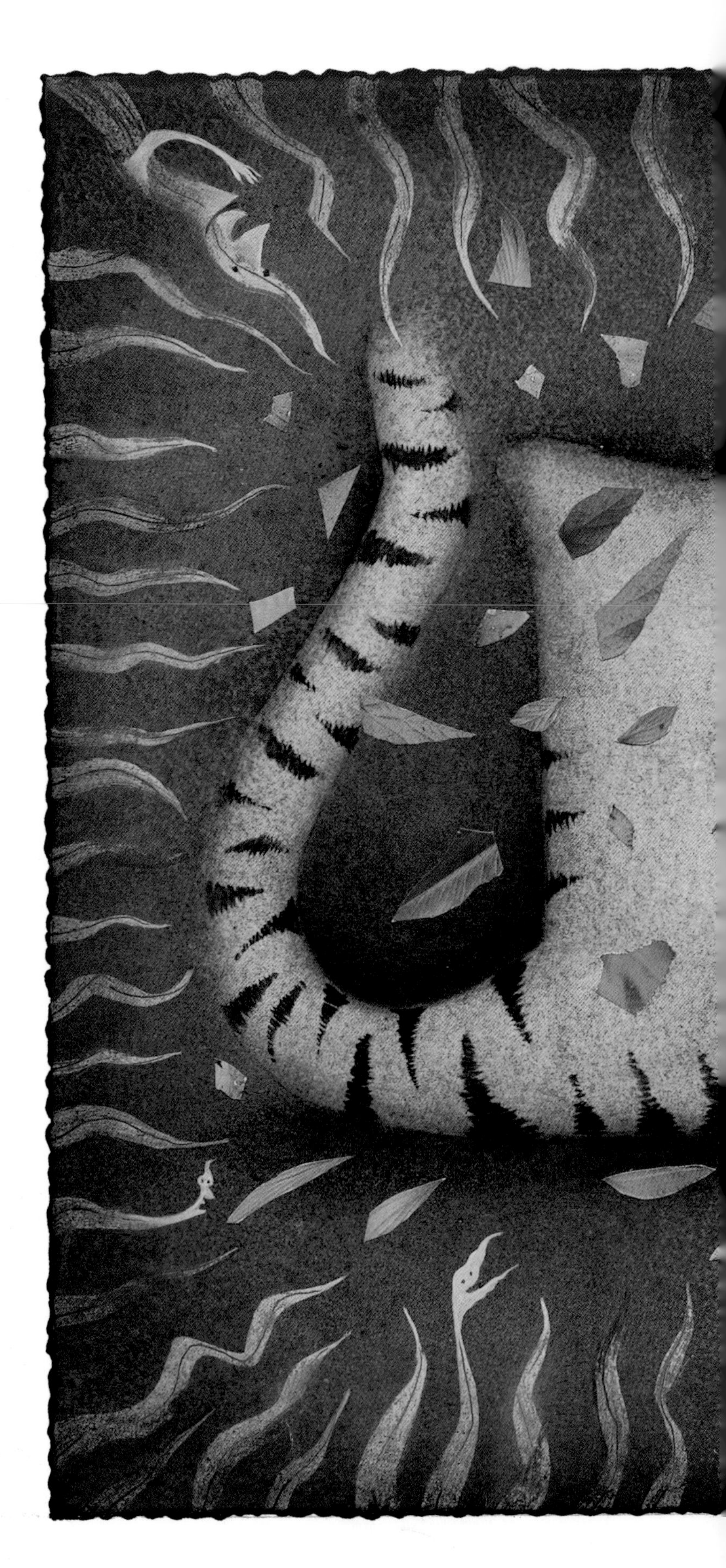

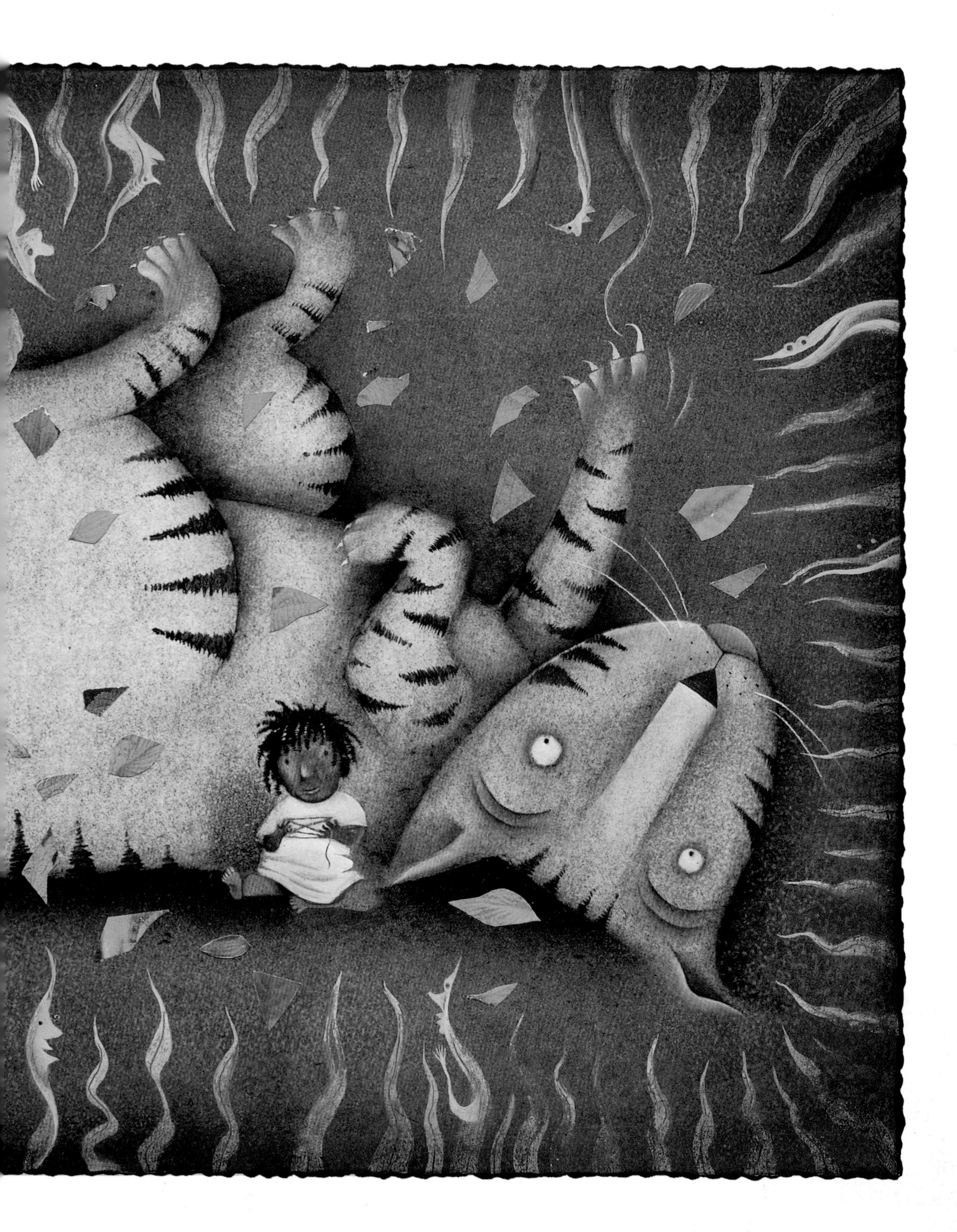

. . . AN ENTIRE MILKY WAY.

Quebec
Montreal
Boston
New York
Bermudas
Chicago
Washington
Charlestown
New Orleans
Bahamas
West
Austin
Galveston
G. of Mexico
Havana
Cuba
Caribbean S.
Windward
Leeward
Jamaica
Tampico
Mexico
Belize
Central
America
Panama
Venezuela
Caracas
Bogota
Colombia
Quito
Ecuador
S. Salvador
Guatemala
L. Nicaragua

The girl was small

and the cat was big.

And their nights always ended in the sleeping basket
that was just big enough for both of them.